The
Babysitting
Wars

candY APPLe books...
Just for you.
sweet. Fresh. Fun.
Take a bite!

The Babysitting Wars

by MIMI McCOY

candy
apple

SCHOLASTIC INC.

New York Toronto London Auckland Sydney
Mexico City New Delhi Hong Kong Buenos Aires

No part of this publication may be reproduced, stored in a retrieval system, or transmitted in any form or by any means, electronic, mechanical, photocopying, recording, or otherwise, without written permission of the publisher. For information regarding permission, write to Scholastic Inc., Attention: Permissions Department, 557 Broadway, New York, NY 10012.

ISBN-13: 978-0-439-92954-7
ISBN-10: 0-439-92954-7

Book design by Tim Hall

12   13 14 15/0
Printed in the U.S.A.   40
First printing, November 2007

For Elyse, with thanks

Chapter One

"Victory!" Kaitlyn Sweeney declared. She strode up to the table in the Marshfield Lake Middle School cafeteria, the fingers of her left hand raised over her head in a *V*.

Her best friends, Liesel and Maggie, looked up from their lunches. Liesel flipped her shaggy blond bangs out of her eyes. "What victory?" she asked.

"I got the last brownie." Kaitlyn held up a walnut-studded square wrapped in plastic.

"Ew, nuts," Liesel said, wrinkling her nose.

Kaitlyn dropped her lunch tray on the table and slid into the seat across from Liesel. "I saw this guy looking at it, so I pretended I was just reaching for a milk. Then, at the last second, I snagged it from right under his nose."

Maggie rolled her eyes. "Kaitlyn, only you could turn buying a brownie into a competitive sport."

"Hey, you snooze, you lose." Kaitlyn unwrapped the brownie. "Anybody want a bite?"

Liesel shook her head. "Walnuts are vile." She'd always been a picky eater. For as long as Kaitlyn had known her — which was pretty much their whole lives — she'd lived mainly on grilled cheese sandwiches and root beer.

"Your loss," Kaitlyn said with a shrug.

"I'll take some," said Maggie, reaching for the brownie.

"Hey, I said a *bite*!"

"Vat wuff a bide," Maggie mumbled through a mouthful.

Maggie was the opposite of Liesel — she ate anything. While Liesel was small, Maggie was tall. She had long black hair that she wore in a braid down her back. Maggie played volleyball and ran on the track and cross-country teams. She had practice every day, and as a result she was *always* hungry.

Kaitlyn was right in between her friends: medium size, medium height, medium-length medium-brown hair. She sometimes joked that the three of them were the perfect set — they came with one in every size.

Kaitlyn polished off the rest of her brownie, then started on a turkey sandwich. Liesel was halfheartedly nibbling at a plate of french fries, and Maggie was working on her second slice of pizza. As she chewed, Kaitlyn glanced around the cafeteria. The sounds of kids' voices bounced off the walls, and the room seemed charged with energy. *Maybe because it's Friday,* Kaitlyn thought. Everyone was excited about the coming weekend.

"Do you guys want to sleep over tomorrow night?" Liesel asked her friends. "My mom has a faculty party at the college, so she won't be home until late. She said we can order pizza."

"I'm in," said Maggie.

"I can't," said Kaitlyn. "I'm babysitting."

"Again?" Liesel heaved an exaggerated sigh.

Kaitlyn looked at her. "What?"

"It's just, you're *always* babysitting lately," Liesel said. "You babysat last Friday *and* last Saturday and the Saturday before that and the Saturday before *that.*"

Kaitlyn couldn't deny it. Just six months before, at the beginning of seventh grade, she'd started babysitting for a few of her mom's friends. Word got out, and suddenly Kaitlyn had more babysitting jobs than she could keep up with.

"Well, I can't cancel now," Kaitlyn replied. "I already told them I'd do it."

"I just don't understand why you want to do it in the first place," Liesel said. "Who wants to sit around wiping little kids' noses? Yech!"

"I do it for the stimulating intellectual conversation," Kaitlyn told her. "And the snacks." Her friends laughed.

"Well, are we all still hanging out at my house tonight?" Maggie asked.

"I'm sitting for the Knopfskys right after school," Kaitlyn said, "but I'll be done pretty early. I can be over by seven." She took another bite of her sandwich.

"Good," said Maggie. "You guys have to see this new video game my brother sent me from college. You build a *mall*. Isn't that cool? You get to pick all the stores but you can't make them all clothes stores, even if you want to, because it turns out a mall won't work with just clothes stores and . . ."

Maggie went on talking. But Kaitlyn no longer heard what she was saying, because at that moment she saw Topher Walker get up from the table where he was sitting with the other basketball players.

Topher Walker, star of the eighth-grade basketball team and owner of the dreamiest set of blue-green eyes Kaitlyn had ever seen, was walking toward their table. And he was looking right at her!

Topher approached, his lips curled in a half smile. Kaitlyn had stopped chewing. In fact, she had pretty much stopped breathing.

"Hey," said Topher.

"Hey," Kaitlyn tried to say. But her mouth was still full of turkey sandwich. It came out "haw."

She felt her face go hot with embarrassment. But Topher didn't seem to notice. He continued past her to the vending machines. Over the noise of the cafeteria, Kaitlyn could hear his coins clatter into the slot of a machine.

Kaitlyn began to breathe again. The bite of sandwich had turned into a gluelike paste in her mouth. She swallowed with difficulty.

"Hello!" Liesel snapped her fingers in front of Kaitlyn's face. "Earth to Kaitlyn."

"Huh?" said Kaitlyn.

Maggie glanced past Kaitlyn at Topher. "Give her a chance to recover," she advised Liesel. "She just had another close encounter of the Topher kind."

"He's like Kaitlyn kryptonite," Liesel noted.

"He is not. Don't look! He'll think we're talking about him," Kaitlyn hissed.

"So? We *are* talking about him," said Liesel. But to Kaitlyn's relief, her friends stopped looking.

Kaitlyn made a face. "Did I really just show him a whole mouthful of chewed turkey?"

"It was only half chewed," Liesel said, as if that somehow made it better.

"Whatever. Not like I really care," Kaitlyn said.

Liesel and Maggie rolled their eyes.

"I don't know why you don't just admit it," Liesel said. "You've got it bad for Topher."

"I do not," said Kaitlyn. "Just because I think he's cute and smart and great at basketball doesn't mean I *like* him. I mean, it's not like I want to go out with him."

"Ri-i-ight," Liesel said.

"He's always trying to be the best," Kaitlyn went on. "Like in Spanish class, whenever Señora Ramos puts challenge words up on the board, he always tries to beat everyone else to answer them."

Maggie and Liesel started laughing.

"What?" said Kaitlyn.

"That sounds just like you," Liesel told her.

"You're perfect for each other," Maggie teased, her eyes twinkling.

Kaitlyn frowned and folded her arms across her chest. Maybe she did like Topher. But she wasn't going to admit it now. She hated to lose a debate.

Before she could say anything else, Maggie

Kaitlyn gave a miniscule shrug in reply.

"Anyway," Maggie said quickly, "Kaitlyn is an amazing babysitter. You should see her at the elementary school. She's practically a celebrity over there."

"Yeah." Kaitlyn laughed. "The Wiggles have got nothing on me."

To Kaitlyn's surprise, Nola's face lit up. "Really? I babysit, too!"

"Oh yeah?" Kaitlyn looked at her with new interest. She didn't think Nola could be a very good babysitter. She looked like she didn't like to get messy.

"I just love little kids," Nola gushed.

Kaitlyn nodded. "Yeah, the kids are cute. And," she added, giving Liesel a meaningful look, "it's a good way to *save* money."

Liesel rolled her eyes. "I'm working on it!"

Nola glanced from one to the other, looking confused.

"We're saving up for a trip to Wonder World," Maggie explained.

"What's Wonder World?" Nola asked.

The three girls stared at her. "You've never heard of Wonder World?" Kaitlyn asked, aghast.

"Wow, you really *aren't* from around here," said Liesel. "Wonder World is . . ."

"'Five acres of pure fun!'" Kaitlyn and Maggie chimed in, quoting from the TV commercial.

"No, really," Liesel said, "it's this huge amusement park about three hours away from here. It's got the biggest roller coaster in ten states!"

"Anyway, we've been wanting to go *forever*," said Maggie.

"At least since fifth grade," said Kaitlyn. "And my mom finally agreed to take us. Only we have to save up the money." She nudged Liesel with her foot.

"I'm working on it!" Liesel repeated. "Don't worry, I have lots of ideas for saving money."

"Name one," Kaitlyn demanded.

"Well, see these quarters?" Liesel held up two coins. "I'm *not* going to spend them on a soda. Instead, I'm going to put them in my pocket and *save* them."

"That's not enough for a soda, anyway," Kaitlyn pointed out.

"All the more reason to save them," Liesel said. She tucked the quarters into the front pocket of her jeans.

"Well, it's a start," Kaitlyn allowed.

Liesel crumpled up her lunch bag and tossed it into a trash can. Then she turned to Kaitlyn and blinked innocently. "Can I borrow some money for a Coke?"

"Liesel!"

"Pretty please, with whipped cream and a cherry on top?"

"I'm serious!" Kaitlyn said. But she was laughing. So was Maggie. Nola smiled uncertainly.

With a pointed sigh, Kaitlyn reached into her pocket and took out some change.

"*Thank you,* Kaitlyn," Liesel singsonged. She took the quarters and skipped over to the vending machine.

"So," said Maggie, turning back to Nola, "what amusement parks do you have in L.A.?"

"Well," Nola began, "I don't really —"

She was interrupted by an electronic jingling. Kaitlyn quickly pulled her cell phone from her pocket and turned off the ringer before the lunchroom monitor could hear it.

"Nice phone," Nola said.

Kaitlyn smiled. The cell phone had been her first major purchase with her babysitting money. She was the only one of her friends who had one.

"I used to have the same one, until I upgraded." Nola whipped out her cell phone. It was the same brand as Kaitlyn's, but a newer model. She flipped it open and showed Kaitlyn the picture on the screen. "Look, that's my dog. Isn't he cute?"

There was something about the proud tilt of

11

Nola's chin that Kaitlyn didn't like. "Excuse me," she said. "I need to get this."

As the other girls continued their conversation, Kaitlyn turned her body slightly away and answered the phone. "Hello?"

"Kaitlyn! Thank goodness you picked up." It was Mrs. Bailey, one of her best customers. "I'm so glad I reached you. We have a bit of a babysitting emergency. Mr. Bailey got invited to dinner with the partners at his firm — he's up for a promotion, you know — and we really need a sitter tonight."

"Did you say *tonight*?" Kaitlyn put her hand over her free ear to try to block out noise from the cafeteria. "I'm really sorry, Mrs. Bailey, but I'm busy tonight."

"Oh no. Are you sure? We only need you for a few hours — maybe from five to eight? You know, Kaitlyn, you're our favorite sitter."

"Thanks, Mrs. Bailey, but —"

"This is very important to us. I'll pay you *double* your normal price."

"Wow. I really wish I could. I'm sorry, Mrs. Bailey." Kaitlyn really *was* sorry. Double her normal price was a lot of money.

"Oh. Well, thanks, anyway, Kaitlyn." Mrs. Bailey sounded positively crushed.

"I hope you find someone," said Kaitlyn. "Bye, Mrs. Bailey."

Kaitlyn hung up and turned back to her friends. Liesel had returned with her soda, and now she and Nola were debating whether loop-de-loop roller coasters were scarier than regular up-and-down roller coasters.

Kaitlyn only half listened. She was still thinking about the offer Mrs. Bailey had just made. *Double* her normal price. That would mean *twice* as much money for Wonder World.

Kaitlyn was certain Maggie would come through with the money for their trip. Even though Maggie didn't have a job like Kaitlyn's, she was saving all her allowance and birthday money.

It was Liesel Kaitlyn was worried about. As far as she knew, Liesel had now saved a grand total of fifty cents, and the trip was only a few months away. At this rate, there was no way she would have enough saved in time. But they couldn't go without Liesel. It wouldn't be the same.

Liesel might not have any way to earn money, Kaitlyn thought. *But I do.*

Kaitlyn began to calculate. She could help pay for Liesel's trip, at least until Liesel could pay her back. It would mean that she'd have to save twice as much. So that's what she would do — starting today.

There was just one problem: the Knopfskys. She was already scheduled to babysit for them that afternoon. Kaitlyn didn't like to think about canceling at the last minute. She prided herself on being reliable.

I'll only do it this one time, she told herself. *We need the money, and this deal is just too good to pass up.*

She started to form her plan. She'd call the Knopfskys and tell them . . . tell them what?

"I'm sick," Kaitlyn murmured.

"You're sick?" Maggie's voice jolted her out of her thoughts. "Really? What's wrong?"

Kaitlyn blinked. Maggie, Liesel, and Nola were all staring at her.

"No, no." Kaitlyn shook her head. "Sorry. I was just thinking aloud."

"Well, come on, then," said Maggie. "The bell just rang."

Kaitlyn stood up from the table. "You guys go ahead. I have to make a phone call."

"I'll wait for you," said Liesel.

"No, really. Go ahead," Kaitlyn said. "I'm right behind you."

Kaitlyn slipped out the side door of the cafeteria. It was a gray, drizzly March day, the kind that made Kaitlyn think spring would never come. The rain had whittled the snow in the school yard down to sad, wet lumps.

She found the Knopfskys' number in her phone and dialed. Kaitlyn licked her lips, feeling nervous. She had never lied to a customer before.

"Hello, Mrs. Knopfsky? It's Kaitlyn," she said. Her voice cracked a little. She hoped that was a good thing. Maybe it would make her sound sicker.

"Hi, Kaitlyn," said Mrs. Knopfsky. "How are you? The kids are looking forward to seeing you this afternoon."

"Well, that's the thing. I'm really sorry, but . . ." Kaitlyn took a deep breath. "I don't think I can make it. I'm not feeling so good. I think I'm coming down with something."

"That's too bad." Mrs. Knopfsky sounded truly concerned. "What do you think it is?"

"Uh . . . I don't know," Kaitlyn mumbled. *Think of something!* she told herself. "I'm super tired. And I have this really, really sore throat." She tried to make her voice sound hoarse, like it was painful to talk.

"Oh no! You certainly should stay home. Do you know anyone else who could sit on short notice?"

Kaitlyn wished she'd thought of that. Instead of canceling, she should have asked Liesel or Maggie to take the job for her. But Maggie had volleyball practice after school, and Liesel claimed she hated to babysit.

"No, I'm sorry. I don't," Kaitlyn said.

"Well, we'll figure something out. Thank you for calling. And feel better." Mrs. Knopfsky hung up.

Kaitlyn leaned against the outside wall of the cafeteria and took a deep breath. Lying felt worse than she'd thought it would — especially since Mrs. Knopfsky had been so nice. But the worst was over. She only had one more call to make.

She scrolled back through her recent calls and dialed.

"Hello, Mrs. Bailey? It's Kaitlyn Sweeney. Guess what! It looks like I can sit for you after all!"

Chapter Two

Kaitlyn sighed and glanced at the DVD player. The digital clock read 9:26. The Baileys were almost an hour and a half late getting home.

She got up from the sofa. In her socks, she quietly crept down the hall to check on Rosie. The little girl was asleep in her bed, hands up alongside her ears, her lips parted in a tiny *O*. Kaitlyn tucked the blanket more tightly around her. She tiptoed out of the room, leaving the door slightly ajar.

Back in the living room, she flopped down on the sofa. With a jingle of dog tags, the Baileys' dachshund, Brutus, hopped up next to her. Kaitlyn patted his head. Brutus was one of the main reasons she liked sitting for the Baileys. She had always wanted a dog, but her father was allergic.

Kaitlyn picked up the television remote and began to flip through channels. Cop show. TV movie. Wrestling. News. Boring. Boring. Boring. Boring.

Kaitlyn glanced at the clock again. 9:29.

Each minute is more money, she reminded herself.

Still, she felt antsy. Even if the Baileys walked in the door that second, it would be too late to go over to Maggie's house. She'd missed yet another night with her friends. It seemed like she'd missed a lot of them lately.

Not that she was complaining. After all, how many other seventh graders had jobs? And she had to admit, she loved it when she went to the park or the grocery store and little kids screamed her name like she was some kind of celebrity.

No, she told herself, babysitting was definitely a good thing. She just sometimes wished she could spend as much time with her friends as she used to.

She continued to channel surf until she found a movie. It was one she'd seen before and she thought it was kind of dumb. But the main actor was cute. He reminded her a little of Topher.

Topher. Kaitlyn cringed, recalling their encounter earlier that day. Had he really not noticed that mouthful of mulched turkey sandwich she'd shown him, or was he just too nice to say anything?

Do I like Topher? Kaitlyn wondered, remembering her conversation with Liesel and Maggie at lunch. There was no question that he was crushworthy. But Topher barely seemed to notice Kaitlyn. They hadn't said more than about three different words all year. Kaitlyn had been counting. Mostly it had been "hey," though there was the occasional "hi," and once, when Topher was passing back a stack of papers in Spanish class, "here." Kaitlyn was no expert, but you didn't need to be a genius to figure out that "hey" plus "hi" plus "here" did not add up to the language of love.

The way Kaitlyn saw it, if she liked Topher and Topher didn't even register her existence, then she was in a losing situation. And Kaitlyn preferred winning situations. In fact, she just preferred winning.

So the only conclusion she could possibly draw was that she didn't like Topher.

He sure is cute, though, Kaitlyn thought with a sigh. She remembered the way he had smiled at her in the cafeteria.

A key scraped in the lock, and the front door opened. Kaitlyn leaped up from the sofa.

"We're home!" Mrs. Bailey said in a loud whisper, coming into the room.

Kaitlyn put a hand to her cheek. She was blushing as if Topher had actually been there. Not that she would ever have a boy over. That was the number one rule of babysitting: no boys in the house.

"I'm sorry we're so late," Mr. Bailey told Kaitlyn as Mrs. Bailey went to check on Rosie. "The dinner lasted much longer than we expected."

"It's okay," said Kaitlyn.

Mrs. Bailey came back into the room, looking satisfied. "Sound asleep," she said.

Kaitlyn nodded. "I heated up that lasagna for her dinner, and then we played with the blocks for a while and I read her *Goodnight Moon*. She went to bed about seven-thirty. Oh, and Rosie's grandmother called. I left the message on the notepad next to the phone."

Kaitlyn had discovered that parents wanted to know every detail, down to which storybooks she read their kids at bedtime. So she always gave a full report. She considered it her trademark.

"You're the best, Kaitlyn," said Mr. Bailey.

Kaitlyn smiled.

Mrs. Bailey took her wallet out of her purse and plucked several bills from inside. "Here you go," she said, handing them to Kaitlyn. "We really appreciate you coming on such short notice."

"It's my pleasure," Kaitlyn said. She folded the money and put it in her pocket. The wad of bills made a lump in her jeans.

"I'll give you a lift," Mrs. Bailey said. "Are you still going to your friend's house?"

Kaitlyn glanced at the DVD clock. 9:59. Much too late to go over to Maggie's.

"That's okay, Mrs. Bailey," she said. "You can just take me home."

Chapter Three

Saturday morning, Kaitlyn was talking to Maggie on her cell and eating cereal straight out of the box, when her call waiting beeped.

"Hold on, Maggie," said Kaitlyn, "there's another call coming in." She switched to the other line.

"Kaitlyn?" said a man's voice.

"Speaking."

"Kaitlyn, hi. It's Mr. Brown."

"Hi, Mr. Brown!" Kaitlyn chirped. The Browns were the people she was sitting for that night. Kaitlyn liked sitting for the Browns. Their kids were pretty well behaved, not to mention they had premium cable and good snacks.

"We just wanted to check in and see how you're feeling," Mr. Brown said.

"I feel fine," Kaitlyn said.

"Really? We saw the Knopfskys last night and they told us how sick you were."

Dang! Kaitlyn had forgotten that the Knopfskys and the Browns were best friends. "Oh, I'm feeling much better," she said hoarsely, trying to sound as if she was recovering from a cold. "Don't worry. I'll be there at six o'clock sharp."

"Oh no, no!" Mr. Brown said quickly. "Don't worry about us. We've already found another sitter."

Double dang! "I don't mind. I really do feel better."

"You need to stay home and get lots of rest. It takes a while to shake this sort of thing."

"If you're sure . . ." Kaitlyn said weakly.

"Sure as sure can be. Feel better, Kaitlyn."

"Okay, well, thanks, Mr. Brown."

Kaitlyn could've kicked herself. Her plan for doubling her pay had just backfired. She'd told a big fat lie, and for what? Now she was just breaking even.

As she got off the phone, it occurred to her to wonder who was sitting for the Browns. But before she could ask, Mr. Brown had hung up.

Later that afternoon, Kaitlyn rode her bike through the slushy streets to Liesel's house. Even though it was light out, the streetlights were starting to come on. Kaitlyn pedaled faster. She wasn't supposed to be riding after dark.

At the end of her road, she turned left onto Lakeside Drive. Marshfield Lake, the suburb Kaitlyn and her friends lived in, was built around a man-made lake. Kaitlyn lived on one side of the lake, Liesel lived on the other, and Maggie lived in between. Kaitlyn had always thought Marshfield Lake was a funny name. It sounded like three different places: marsh, field, lake. But there were no marshes or fields in Marshfield Lake. "Marshfield" came from Henry Marshfield, the developer who'd built most of the houses in their town. He had died before Kaitlyn was born, but his son and his son's family lived in a big mansion on a hill overlooking the lake.

Kaitlyn had never met the Marshfields, but she'd seen them riding through town in a chauffeured Mercedes-Benz. She'd heard they had two kids, but Kaitlyn didn't know how old the kids were. They had a live-in nanny, so they didn't need a babysitter.

As Kaitlyn coasted up the alley that led to the back of Liesel's house, Liesel came darting out the door. She was wearing galoshes and an extra-large sweatshirt over a pair of leggings.

"You can't come in this way," Liesel said, heading her off. "The painting is drying in the kitchen. You'll have to go around to the front of the house."

For weeks, Liesel had been working on her painting for the youth art show. She wouldn't let anyone see it, not even her mother. Everyone was on strict instructions to stay out of the kitchen when Liesel was working.

Kaitlyn parked her bike at the back of the house, then trudged through the melting snow around to the front door.

Liesel met her there. "Maggie's up in my room," she said. "I'll bring some drinks up. The painting will be dry in a while, and then I can move it."

As Liesel headed off to the kitchen, Kaitlyn climbed the stairs to Liesel's room. Most of the houses in Marshfield Lake had the same floor plan, give or take a few rooms. It was possible to go into a total stranger's house and still know exactly where their bathroom and kitchen and coat closet were. Liesel's room was in the same place as Kaitlyn's room was in her house — on the southwest-facing side.

The similarity ended at the door, however. Whereas Kaitlyn had the same peach-colored walls and matching floral bedspread she'd had since first grade, Liesel's walls were covered with her sketches and paintings. Kaitlyn couldn't remember what Liesel's bedspread looked like, because the bed was always buried under clothes.

"Look out! Babysitter on the loose!" Maggie cried as Kaitlyn walked through the door. "There's no telling what this diaper-changing daredevil might do on her night off."

Kaitlyn grinned. Maggie was curled up in an overstuffed chair. Her long hair framed her face like a curtain.

Kaitlyn moved a pile of clothes and sat down on the bed. "You know, I was bummed about it before, but now I'm actually kind of glad my babysitting job got canceled. I'm psyched to have a night just to hang out." She didn't bother to go into the whole story of how she'd tried to double her money for Liesel's sake. Somehow she didn't think Maggie would approve.

"Speaking of babysitting, look what I found at the supermarket." Maggie reached into her back pocket and pulled out a folded square of bright yellow paper. She handed it to Kaitlyn.

Kaitlyn unfolded it. "'Need a babysitter?'" she read. "'Call Nola for the best in professional babysitting! The latest techniques in child care. Excellent references. Educational games and organic snacks provided.' And here's her number. Is this . . . ?"

Maggie nodded. "The new girl. It must be. I mean, how many people are named Nola?"

Kaitlyn studied the flyer. "She's charging a dollar less than me. And what does 'the latest techniques in child care' mean?"

"I don't know. But I'm sure she's got nothing on you," said Maggie. "Everyone knows you're the best babysitter in town."

"Yeah," said Kaitlyn. Still, she felt a spark of annoyance. Educational games? Organic snacks? Whatever.

Kaitlyn crumpled up the flyer and threw it in the trash.

"Dinner is served," Liesel said from the doorway. She held up three cans of root beer. "Just kidding," she added, seeing Maggie's horrified look. She tossed a can to Maggie and came to sit next to Kaitlyn on the bed.

Maggie tapped her fingernails on the top of the can to settle the bubbles. "So what do you guys want to do tonight?"

"We could play Monopoly," Kaitlyn suggested.

"No!" Maggie and Liesel shouted.

"It was just a suggestion," Kaitlyn said defensively. She loved Monopoly, but she could never get her friends to play with her, just because *one time* she'd thrown the board out the window when she was losing. It was totally unfair. For Pete's sake, that had been over a year ago!

"We could order pizza," Maggie said.

"Pizza!" Kaitlyn seconded.

Liesel picked up her phone. "Pepperoni?"

"With olives," said Kaitlyn.

"With mushrooms," said Maggie.

"With olives and mushrooms," said Kaitlyn.

Liesel made a face. She dialed the number of the pizza place. "Hi, a large pizza for delivery? Pepperoni, with olives and mushrooms *on half*." She gave them her address and phone number and hung up.

"How are you going to keep up your strength for the art show if you don't eat your vegetables?" Kaitlyn teased.

"Root beer *is* a vegetable," Liesel replied. "It's a root."

"I can't wait for the show," Maggie gushed. "What are you going to wear, Liesel? You have to look super glamorous."

Liesel shrugged. "No, I don't. I'm an artist, not a fashion model."

"But it's your big debut!" Maggie protested.

"So I'll look like an artist. This is what artists look like." Liesel gestured toward her paint-splattered sweatshirt.

"Come on. Everyone likes to look good." Kaitlyn got up and went over to the closet. "There's got to be something in here." She yanked a silky dress off a hanger. "What about this?"

Liesel snorted. "That's a bathrobe."

Kaitlyn took a closer look. "Oh yeah. It's kind of pretty, though." She slipped it over her sweater and jeans and twirled around. "Maybe people will think it's a kimono."

"Try again," said Maggie.

Kaitlyn plunged her hands back into the closet. She came up with a denim dress that snapped up the front.

"That fit great . . . in fifth grade," said Liesel.

Kaitlyn studied it. "How come you never wore it in fifth grade?"

"I did once, remember? I was climbing on the jungle gym at recess and that jerk Branson Farley made fun of my skinny legs."

"Ohhhhh," Kaitlyn and Maggie said, remembering. Kaitlyn put the dress back into the closet.

She flipped through the rest of the clothes on the hangers. "Flannel, flannel, hoodie, thermal, down vest, thermal . . . oh, and these." She held up a pair of jeans that had been patched in so many places there was hardly any denim left.

"I've been looking for those!" Liesel cried. "I wonder how they got in the closet?"

Kaitlyn shut the closet door. "Well, you may have to go in that sweatshirt after all. You definitely do not have any fancy clothes."

"What about your mom?" Maggie asked. "My mom has all these old dresses in the back of her closet, stuff that doesn't fit her anymore. She never throws away anything."

Liesel thought for a moment. "There's some old stuff in the closet of the wreck room."

"Let's check it out," Kaitlyn said, setting down her soda.

The wreck room was just down the hall from Liesel's room. It was called that because it always looked like a hurricane had recently been through. Broken furniture competed for space with empty bottles, egg cartons, jars of old paintbrushes, piles of magazines, short-circuited appliances, dusty baskets of plastic fruit, and anything else that Liesel and her mother couldn't bring themselves to throw away.

Kaitlyn opened the closet door. "How do you find anything in here?" she asked.